ff

BERTIE BOGGIN
AND THE
GHOST AGAIN!

Catherine Sefton

illustrated by Jill Bennett

faber and faber
LONDON · BOSTON

First published in 1988 by
Faber and Faber Limited
3 Queen Square London WC1N 3AU

Phototypeset by Wilmaset Birkenhead Wirral
Printed in Great Britain by
Richard Clay Ltd Bungay Suffolk

Text © Catherine Sefton, 1988
Illustrations © Faber and Faber Limited, 1988

British Library Cataloguing in Publication Data

Sefton, Catherine
Bertie Boggin and the ghost again!
Rn: Martin Waddell I. Title
823'.914 [J] PZ7
ISBN 0–571–15124–8

For Phyllis Hunt
with many thanks

Contents

Chapter One

Big News for the Boggins

Bertie Boggin's best friend was the Ghost who lived in the coal shed at the back of his house, in Livermore Street, Belfast.

Nobody else believed in the Ghost, except Mrs Boggin *sometimes*, and so nobody else could see him. Bertie's brother Max and his sister Elsie and Mr Boggin went round saying there *was* no Ghost, but that didn't bother Bertie, who knew better. Tojo, the dog, sniffed *ghost* now and then, and found it all very confusing.

One day, Mrs Boggin put on her coat and hat and went to the doctor's, and when she came back home she was bright red in the face, and very happy.

She went round the house singing:

> I'M H–A–P–P–Y
> I'M H–A–P–P–Y
> I'M
> H–A–P–P–Y!

so loudly that the Ghost pulled his hat down over his

ears and skedaddled out to the coal shed, where he could rest in peace.

'What's Mum so happy about?' asked Max.

'Don't know!' said Elsie.

'I'll ask her!' said Bertie.

So he did.

'What are you being H–A–P–P–Y about, Mum?' asked Bertie.

'Big news!' said Mrs Boggin.

'How big?' said Bertie. 'This big?' and he made the biggest shape he could with his hands.

'Bigger than that!' said Mrs Boggin cheerfully.

'Big–big–big news?' said Bertie.

'The biggest!' said Mrs Boggin. 'Wait until your father gets home, and you'll hear all about it.'

Bertie told Max and Elsie.

'Big–big–big news!' said Bertie. 'Big as an elephant, almost!' An elephant was the biggest thing he knew about, so he thought it must be elephant-big news, if it was the biggest.

'What *sort* of big news?' asked Max.

'Maybe it *is* an elephant,' said Elsie. 'I bet that's what it is. Daddy's coming home with an elephant, especially for Bertie.'

'Is he?' said Bertie.

'*Probably*,' said Max.

'An E–L–E–P–H–A–N–T!' said Bertie excitedly, and he rushed out to the back yard to tell the Ghost about it.

The Ghost was fast asleep on his stack of coal at the time, under his hat.

Bertie woke him up by banging on it.

'Wake up, Ghost! Wake up!' Bertie shouted.

'Eh . . . ah . . . OH!' yawned the Ghost; then he opened his eyes and blinked at Bertie. He had been dreaming about far-away days, with Florence Nightingale at flower shows, and he wasn't very pleased at having his hat rudely knocked.

'Wake up – wake up – wake up!' shouted Bertie.

'I am awake,' said the Ghost, putting his knocked-on hat straight.

'I'm getting an elephant,' said Bertie.

'What?' said the Ghost.

'Daddy's bringing home an elephant,' said Bertie.

The Ghost thought about it. 'Are you sure, Bertie?' he asked.

'A big–big–big one, just for me!' said Bertie.

'I used to ride elephants,' said the Ghost. 'Great clumsy things, that eat buns.'

'Do they?' said Bertie.

'Yes,' said the Ghost. 'You ride on top of them and they eat buns and they squirt people sometimes, with their trunks. Ghosts are fond of elephants, because they can see elephants coming a long way off, and get out of the way.'

'I don't want to get out of the elephant's way!' said Bertie. 'I'm going to ride it to school, *every* day! I'll be the only one in P2 with an elephant, if my Daddy brings one home.'

'Perhaps the elephant will bring Daddy home,' said the Ghost.

'I don't care which!' said Bertie.

'You would if you were your Daddy,' said the Ghost. 'Riding home on top of an elephant is one thing; an elephant riding home on top of your Daddy would be quite another.'

'I expect Daddy will ride it home,' said Bertie. 'I expect he'll get one from the Zoo. Don't you?'

'I suppose he might,' said the Ghost, looking round the yard at Livermore Street, and beginning to wonder where the elephant would go. It wouldn't fit in the coal shed, and it wouldn't fit under the stairs.

'I wonder where he'll put it?' the Ghost said.

'In my room!' said Bertie.

'I don't think . . .' the Ghost began, but Bertie wasn't there. He had run off upstairs to get his room ready for the big–big–big elephant.

Max and Elsie were playing Doctor Who's Monsters on the landing, when they heard a lot of bumping in Bertie's room.

Max looked round the door.

Bertie was trying to move his bed.

'What are you moving your bed for, Bertie?' said Max.

'To make room for the elephant,' said Bertie.

'Oh yes,' said Max. 'I see. The *Elephant*.'

'If I move the bed, and my chair, there *ought* to be enough room for my elephant,' said Bertie.

'If it is a small one,' said Elsie.

'It isn't,' said Bertie. 'It's big–big–big.'

5

'Then you might have to move out of your room,' said
Max unkindly. 'I wonder where Mum will put you?'
　'Out in the back yard, with his ghost!' giggled Elsie.
　'Will she?' said Bertie.
　'Only place I can think of,' said Max.
　'Certain to,' said Elsie.
　'You *fit* in the coal shed, Bertie,' said Max. 'Your

elephant wouldn't, would it? Not if it is a great big elephant. So I think you'll have to move into the coal shed with your ghost, and the elephant can sleep in your room.'

'Oh,' said Bertie.

'Better pack up all your things, ready for the move,' said Elsie.

Bertie didn't pack. He stayed in his room for a long time, but he came down for his tea.

'Big Tea today!' said Mr Boggin cheerfully. 'Celebrations!'

'Oh!' said Max. 'Little Sausages!'

'And cherry cake!' said Elsie.

'And buns!' said Mrs Boggin.

'Is it here, then?' asked Bertie anxiously.

'Is what here, Bertie?'

'The elephant the buns are for,' said Bertie.

'What elephant?' said Mrs Boggin.

And Bertie told her.

'Max says I've got to move out of my room and go and live in the coal shed and I don't think there'll be room in the coal shed with my Ghost and couldn't I sleep in the bathroom instead?' said Bertie.

'Max!' said Mr Boggin.

'I didn't say there *was* an elephant,' said Max. 'I just said *if* there was, Bertie *might* have to move *out* of his room to let the elephant *in*. He couldn't share his room with an elephant, could he? I mean . . .'

'*Isn't* there an elephant?' said Bertie.

7

'No, Bertie,' said Mrs Boggin.

'But you said big–big–big . . .' Bertie faltered. 'And . . . and there are buns, aren't there? And elephants eat buns . . .'

'So do boys, Bertie,' said Mrs Boggin.

'And girls!' said Elsie.

'And elephants,' Bertie insisted. 'Elephants eat buns.'

'These buns were not bought for an elephant, Bertie,' said Mrs Boggin. 'They're to celebrate our big news.'

'What big news?' said Max.

'We're . . .' Mr Boggin began, and then he stopped. 'You tell them!' he said to Mrs Boggin.

'Max, Elsie, Bertie,' said Mrs Boggin. 'Today I went to the doctor, and he gave me big–big–big news. And the big–big–big news is . . . we're having a baby!'

There was a long silence.

'What *for*?' said Bertie.

'*For* . . . because we're having one,' said Mrs Boggin. 'A little brother or sister, that you can play with. Won't that be nice?'

'Y-e-s!' said Elsie.

'I think it's soppy,' said Max. 'I don't like soppy babies.'

'Will I . . . will I have to move out of my room?' said Bertie.

'No, Bertie,' said Mrs Boggin.

'Not even if it is a big–big–big baby like an elephant?' said Bertie, who still thought that there might be an elephant somewhere about the house, ready to hop out and finish the buns.

'Absolutely not, Bertie,' said Mrs Boggin.

'I suppose I don't mind, then,' said Bertie.

When the Big News Tea was over, Bertie went outside to tell the Ghost.

'We're not having an elephant, Ghost,' said Bertie. 'We're having a baby instead!'

'Oh, brilliant!' said the Ghost, and he threw his ghostly hat up in the air, and danced round and round on top of the coal.

'*Is* it brilliant?' said Bertie.

'Yes,' said the Ghost. 'One more to play with! A little one. Ghosts have a soft spot for babies.'

'Why?' said Bertie.

'Because most babies believe in ghosts,' said the Ghost. 'It's grown-up people who don't. And ghosts like people who believe in them, because they are the only people ghosts can play with.'

'Like me?' said Bertie.

'Exactly like you!' said the Ghost.

Bertie went back into the house. 'The Ghost is glad we're having a baby, Mum,' he said.

'And I'm glad he's glad, Bertie,' said Mrs Boggin.

'When will we get it?' said Bertie.

'Months and months and months yet, Bertie,' said Mrs Boggin.

'When we get it, can I play with it?' asked Bertie.

'Yes,' said Mrs Boggin. 'When it is big enough to play.'

'And can my Ghost play with it too?' said Bertie.

'Of course, Bertie,' said Mrs Boggin.

'Good,' said Bertie.

'And you tell your Ghost not to worry about the baby, Bertie,' said Mrs Boggin. 'It will only be a wee tiny titchy one to begin with, and it won't disturb him at all.'

Then she took Bertie upstairs and put him to bed in his own little room, with the bed moved back and plenty of room for Bertie in it.

And no room for an elephant, because there wasn't one.

Chapter Two

The Ghost Boast

'Mum,' said Bertie, one day. 'You know the wee tiny titchy baby we're going to get?'

'Yes, Bertie,' said Mrs Boggin.

'Where do we get it?' said Bertie.

'From in me,' said Mrs Boggin. 'Inside my tummy, the wee tiny titchy baby is growing right now, Bertie. And when it gets much much bigger, it will come out, and then it will be our baby.'

'How did it get there?' said Bertie.

'Special magic,' said Mrs Boggin. 'The same sort of special magic that brought you.'

'Was I in your tummy, Mum?' asked Bertie.

'When you were very, very, very small. Before you popped out.'

'Now I'm big,' said Bertie.

'Yes,' said Mrs Boggin. 'You popped out ages and ages ago.'

'And Max? And Elsie too?' said Bertie.

'Yes,' said Mrs Boggin. 'But not all at once.'

'And then the baby will get bigger, like me and Max and Elsie?' said Bertie.

'Yes,' said Mrs Boggin. 'Only meantime you'll be getting bigger too.'

'When will I get big like Max?' said Bertie.

'Soon,' said Mrs Boggin.

'How soon is soon?' Bertie asked.

'As soon as you learn to eat all your dinner every day!' said Mrs Boggin.

'He won't grow big,' said Elsie. 'Just fat!'

'He's fat enough already,' said Max. 'Gi-normous fat, for such a small person.'

'No I'm not,' said Bertie, trying to look thin.

'Small *and* fat,' said Max.

'And ugly!' said Elsie.

'I'll small, fat and ugly you!' said Mrs Boggin. 'Buzz off and stop talking like that, or you'll make Bertie cry.'

Max and Elsie buzzed off, but on the way out of the door Max said: 'Small, fat, ugly cry-baby!' and Mrs Boggin chased him with the wooden spoon.

Bertie went out to the coal shed, to talk to the Ghost.

'I'm not a small, fat, ugly cry-baby, Ghost, am I?' said Bertie, with a sniff, because his eyes were watery.

'Of course not,' said the Ghost. He pretended not to notice the watery eyes, because he was Bertie's Best Friend, and didn't like to see Bertie upset. 'You're not fat, and you're not ugly, and you're *definitely* not a cry-baby!'

'But I am small,' Bertie said.

'Well, a *bit* small,' admitted the Ghost. 'You have to be small first, before you can be big.'

'*You* don't,' Bertie pointed out.

'That's because I'm a Ghost,' explained the Ghost. 'Ghosts need to be small, sometimes, to get in and out of things that other people can't get in and out of.'

'What sort of things?' asked Bertie.

'Keyholes,' said the Ghost, and he wisped through the kitchen keyhole, and out under the door again, just to show Bertie how good he was at it.

'How do you make yourself bigger, Ghost?' Bertie asked.

'I breathe myself up!' said the Ghost, and he took a

big deep breath, and puffed himself up. Then . . . *foooooo* . . . he let out his breath, and shrank himself down again. 'Takes practice, of course,' he said. 'And natural ability. Not everyone can do it. It's easy for me, of course, because I am a very smart ghost.'

'Hmm!' said Bertie, who had his own ideas about boasty-ghosty remarks like that. But still, a few minutes later, when Max and Elsie were in the kitchen, they heard a funny noise from the yard.

'Look, Max!' said Elsie, and Max looked.

Bertie was standing on top of the coal in the coal shed

14

with his cheeks puffed out and his chest stuck forward, like a wrestler.

'If you hold your breath like that, you'll burst!' said Max. 'You'll make a mess all over the coal.'

'Bertie!' cried Elsie. 'Oh Bertie. Don't burst.'

'Go on, burst,' said Max, who had never seen anyone bursting before.

'Mum,' screeched Elsie. 'Bertie's going to burst!'

Bertie knew when he was beaten. He stopped holding his breath. It hadn't done any good at all. He was still the same size, bigger than the baby in Mrs Boggin's tummy, and smaller than Max and Elsie and Tojo.

'Are you all right, Bertie?' Elsie asked anxiously.

'No. He's all wrong, as usual!' said Max.

They went back into the house.

'It doesn't work,' Bertie told the Ghost.

'Not for just anyone,' said the Ghost. 'Ghosts have a talent for it, you know. It takes years and years of practice, haunting in spooky places with locked doors. Not *all* ghosts can manage it, of course. Some ghosts are just beginners. Ghosts that have been around a bit get Extra Specially Good at it. Being bigger is really no problem at all for an experienced ghost, like me.'

'Bertie?' said Mrs Boggin, who had been having a lie-down on the couch. 'Coming to the library with me?'

'Yes please!' said Bertie, who liked the library, because he could look at books there. He was slow at reading, even though he was in P2, but he liked looking.

'Me too!' said the Ghost.

'You don't deserve to come,' Bertie told the Ghost, when they were walking down Ormeau Road behind Mrs Boggin.

'Yes I do,' said the Ghost. 'Libraries are full of stories about interesting people, and ghosts are interesting people, so ghosts feel at home there. There are stories about other ghosts in books, and there are books about people that ghosts used to know, like my friend Florence Nightingale the famous nurse. Ghosts know lots of famous people, especially ghosts who really deserve to be famous themselves because . . .'

'I wish you'd stop boasting!' said Bertie.

'Ghosts deserve a little boast, now and then,' said the Ghost, and then he added: 'They deserve a little boast after all they have to put up with from people who can't even shrink!'

But he said it in a soft voice, so that Bertie wouldn't hear him.

Mrs Boggin and Bertie and the Ghost got to the library.

'Bertie,' said Mrs Boggin. 'I want you to behave yourself and sit on that chair reading while I choose my books. No noise at all. Promise?'

'I promise,' said Bertie, and he sat down on the chair.

The Ghost made himself very very small by breathing in and holding his breath, until he was small enough to sit on Bertie's shoulder, where he could talk into Bertie's ear.

'I've shrunk,' the Ghost told Bertie. 'I told you I could make myself smaller, didn't I? It isn't just blowing myself up big I'm good at, I can be smaller as well. Ghosts can do things like that.'

'Some ghosts have Big Heads!' said Bertie, not sounding very pleased.

'Ghosts need big heads,' said the Ghost. 'Especially ghosts like me with lots of brains to put in them.'

'Please be quiet,' whispered Bertie. 'Mum said not to talk loudly because we're in the library.'

'Libraries are quiet places,' whispered the Ghost. 'Ghosts like quiet places, because quiet places remind them of Peaceful Haunts before T.V. was invented. No stereo. No video. No pop groups. All you got was the occasional battle going on, with cannonballs whizzing and swords clanging and . . .'

'You're talking loudly again!' Bertie said. It was true, because when the Ghost talked about cannonballs and swords and battles he got excited.

'Bertie! Keep quiet! You promised!' said Mrs Boggin.

'I was talking to the Ghost,' Bertie explained.

'Well, don't,' said Mrs Boggin. 'Read a picture book instead.' And she gave Bertie a book about railway engines to read. It was very boring, although the pictures were nice.

'Could you *please* be quiet, Ghost?' whispered Bertie. 'Otherwise you'll get us both into trouble.'

'Shush!' hissed Mrs Boggin.

Bertie opened his mouth, and then he shut it again. If

he wasn't allowed to speak, how could he tell the Ghost to keep quiet? Perhaps, if he whispered very softly . . .

'G–h–o–s–t . . .' began Bertie, but the Ghost had gone.

'Showing off his shrinking again!' thought Bertie. 'Just because he can make himself small, and I can't.'

'Stop showing off, Ghost!' Bertie said, out loud, but there was no reply. Luckily, Mrs Boggin didn't hear him.

She was looking at books in the Name-Your-Baby section. She took one down, and sat at a table with it.

She took ages, looking at baby names.

Bertie was bored. In the end, he got up from his chair and went on a Ghost Hunt, round the library.

He looked around the bookcases, where he thought the Ghost might be playing Ghost Hide and Ghost Seek, but he wasn't. No Ghost.

He looked under three of the reading tables. No Ghost.

He looked in the coatstand and in the Author/Title index under 'G' (for 'Ghost') and he opened a match-box he found under the Librarian's desk, just in case the Ghost had breathed himself very small and hidden inside it.

No Ghost!

T–h–e–n . . .

'Help! Help! *Bertie!* Help!' The muffled voice came from the bookshelf above Bertie's head.

'Ghost?' said Bertie. 'Where are you, Ghost?'

'Trapped inside this big yellow book!' said the voice, sounding upset. The Ghost had been peacefully reading when someone had closed the book with a snap, and placed it back on the shelf.

'Get me out!' the Ghost shouted.

'I can't,' said Bertie. 'You are too high up. I can't reach you. Can't you shrink, and slide out?'

'Not from a closed book!' grumbled the Ghost. 'Blow yourself up, then you'll be able to reach me.'

'You know that only works for Rather Special Ghosts,' said Bertie, not very kindly.

'Do something, Bertie!' wailed the Ghost, who was completely flattened inside the book, without any shrinking room.

'Mum,' said Bertie. 'Mum. Can I see that big yellow book up there?'

Mrs Boggin picked the big yellow book off the shelf and opened it.

'*Haunted Houses of Belfast*,' she read, looking at the first page. 'This isn't a boy's book, Bertie.'

'You can put it back on the shelf now, thank you,' said Bertie, who had seen the Ghost wisp out from between the pages, looking flatter than usual, but unharmed.

'Thank you for rescuing me,' said the Ghost, quickly breathing himself back up to full size, to avoid getting trapped in another book. 'You are a Hero, Bertie. When we get home I will give you a Special Saving-Ghosts-

From-Inside-Books Medal. There aren't many of them, because ghosts don't get caught in books, much.'

'Why not?' asked Bertie.

'Because most ghosts are the wrong size,' said the Ghost. 'Ghosts are usually too big to fit into books . . .'

'Ghosts who *stay the right size* are,' said Bertie. He didn't say anything about ghosts who showed off by blowing themselves up bigger and shrinking themselves down smaller, but the Ghost knew what he was talking about.

The Ghost started talking about something else, quickly.

'It was not a good book,' said the Ghost. 'It doesn't mention Livermore Street, or my coal shed. Imagine calling a book *Haunted Houses of Belfast* and not mentioning my coal shed.'

'Coal sheds don't count as houses,' said Bertie, trying to be helpful.

'They do if you happen to live in one,' said the Ghost, and he went straight off home to have a cup of tea and catch up on the Spook Reviews in the *Evening Haunt*. He was a *comfortable* kind of ghost to have around your coal shed, even if he was big-headed sometimes.

'Mum,' said Bertie. 'How soon is the soon when I'll be a big boy?'

'You're a big boy now,' said Mrs Boggin.

'Not big like Max,' said Bertie.

'No, big like Bertie. You are just about right-sized for you and Max is just about right-sized for Max, and later on you'll be right–sized–for–you–later–on. If you were big now, you'd be wrong-sized for you, and that can get you into lots of trouble.'

'I know,' said Bertie.

'How do you know?' said Mrs Boggin.

'Something like that happened once to a friend of mine,' said Bertie.

But he didn't tell her who it was, because she *might* not have believed him.

Chapter Three

Bertie and the Cow

'Today I am taking Bertie down to the farm at Ballynahinch to visit his Aunt Amanda,' Mrs Boggin announced, one breakfast-time.

'Oh, let us come too, *please*!' said Max, who liked visiting Aunt Amanda Boggin because there was lots of food at her house, like jelly and chips and ice-cream and runny egg.

'No, Max,' said Mrs Boggin. 'You and Elsie are staying at home with your Dad. This is a special treat, just for Bertie and Mummy.'

'And the Ghost,' said Bertie.

'Is he on about that Ghost *again*?' said Mr Boggin, lowering his newspaper.

'Yes!' said Max, hoping Bertie would get into trouble.

'Bertie's got a perfect right to have a Ghost, if he wants one!' said Mrs Boggin quickly.

'I have enough trouble, without ghosts about the place!' grumbled Mr Boggin.

'You're only cross because you'll have Max and Elsie to look after for the day!' said Mrs Boggin.

'Humph!' said Mr Boggin, and he disappeared behind his paper again.

'You're both to be very good, and not annoy your father!' Mrs Boggin told Max and Elsie, and then she dressed Bertie up in his best red jersey and his yellow pants and his wellington boots, in case he stood in anything at the farm.

The Ghost put on his best hat, from under Max's bed, and his balaclava to keep his ears warm, and got into the back seat of the Volkswagen.

'Have a nice day, dear,' said Mrs Boggin, and she kissed Mr Boggin goodbye. 'Be good, Max and Elsie.'

'It isn't fair!' said Elsie. 'We want to go too!'

'Well, you can't,' said Mrs Boggin. 'I've got something very special to discuss with Aunt Amanda, and Bertie and his Ghost are quite enough for me to cope with, while I'm doing it.'

And off she drove in the Volkswagen, with Bertie sitting in the back wearing a jelly and chips and ice-cream and runny egg look on his face, which annoyed Max and Elsie very much.

Bertie had chicken and chips and jelly and runny egg and lemonade and four biscuits at Aunt Amanda's, while his Mum and Aunt Amanda were talking, and then Aunt Amanda and Mrs Boggin took him out to look round the farm.

He saw hens and chicken and tractors and . . .

'A Moo–Moo!' said Aunt Amanda.

'See the nice cow, Bertie,' said Mrs Boggin.

Bertie looked at the nice cow, and the nice cow looked at Bertie.

It was black and white and fat and sad-looking, and it had big brown eyes and a shiny nose.

The cow mooed at Bertie.

'It likes you, Bertie,' said Mrs Boggin. 'The cow likes you.'

'Bertie's Moo–Moo,' said Aunt Amanda. 'We shall call this Moo–Moo Bertie's Special Moo–Moo, shan't we, Bertie?'

'*Cow*,' said Bertie, politely. 'It's a cow.'

'Yes, dear,' said Aunt Amanda, 'but we'll call it your Moo–Moo, won't we?'

'All right,' said Bertie, and he trotted off to tell the Ghost about it.

The Ghost was in the barn, where he was pretending to drive the tractor.

'Zoom–Varoom!' went the Ghost. 'Brrrr–uuuu–zzzz! Aaaaaah! Varooom! Beeeeep! Beep–beep–beep!'

'Ghost?' said Bertie.

'Don't interrupt me when I'm driving, Bertie,' said the Ghost. 'I might crash. Zoom–Varoom! Barooom! BAM!'

'Did you hit something?' said Bertie anxiously.

'Ghosts do not hit things when they are driving, Bertie,' said the Ghost.

'What was the BAM! then?' asked Bertie.

'That was the other drivers hitting each other, trying to get out of my way!' the Ghost explained patiently.

24

'I don't see any other drivers,' Bertie said.

'Sometimes I think you haven't got much imagination, Bertie,' said the Ghost, with dignity. 'Ghosts used to race at Brooklands, you know. I was zooming down the track when . . .'

'Your tractor didn't even move,' said Bertie.

'Tractor?' said the Ghost. 'What tractor?'

'The tractor you weren't driving,' said Bertie. 'I know you *weren't* driving it, because it didn't move.'

'It wasn't being a tractor, Bertie,' said the Ghost. 'It was being a Super-car, like I drove in my racing days. I zoom–varoomed all over the road. I was the best driver ever. I . . .'

'You're boasting again, Ghost,' said Bertie.

'Some ghosts have plenty to boast about, Bertie,' said the Ghost. 'Not like some boys!'

'I've got a cow to boast about,' said Bertie.

'Ah!' said the Ghost. 'Not as good as a racing car, but still. Ghosts like cows, Bertie. Cows don't *often* spring out on ghosts. Not like large dogs. Large dogs are always springing out on ghosts and surprising them. I am glad that you are getting a cow, Bertie. Cows are very sensible. Zooom! Varoom! Beep–beep–beep!' And he drove off again.

Bertie waited politely until the Ghost stopped on the twenty-second lap round the race-course, and then he said: 'Aunt Amanda has given me a real cow. It is just for me. It really is. She says we can call it Bertie's Special Moo–Moo. Moo–Moo is what Aunt Amanda calls cows,' he added apologetically.

'Aunts are sometimes like that, Bertie,' said the Ghost, who had haunted a few Aunts in his time.

'I'm going to take it home to show Max and Elsie,' said Bertie. 'They haven't got cows.'

'Home?' said the Ghost doubtfully.

'Home to my house!' said Bertie proudly, and then he added: 'Our house, I mean,' because the Ghost was looking a bit upset.

'You're not putting it in my coal shed,' said the Ghost, getting down off his tractor.

'Why not?' said Bertie.

'I have nothing *personal* against cows, Bertie,' said the Ghost, glowing slightly at the thought of sharing his home. 'But I do not wish to live with one in my coal shed. Not even a little one. You must put your cow somewhere else.'

'I don't think Mum would let me put it in the kitchen,' said Bertie, sounding worried.

'I think *not*,' said the Ghost.

'Oh,' said Bertie, and he went back to the house, where Mrs Boggin and Aunt Amanda were continuing their Very Special Discussion.

'Where am I going to put my Special Cow?' Bertie asked Mrs Boggin and then he added, for Aunt Amanda's benefit, 'My Special Moo–Moo, I mean.'

'Oh dear!' said Aunt Amanda. 'Oh dear, poor little Bertie.'

'Bertie,' said Mrs Boggin. 'Bertie, let Mummy explain.'

'Explain what?' said Bertie anxiously.

'About your Moo–Moo,' said Mrs Boggin.

'*Cow*,' said Bertie.

'Your cow,' said Mrs Boggin. 'You see, Aunt Amanda didn't mean you to take the cow *away*. Cows live on farms. Cows don't live on the Ormeau Road. Cows wouldn't be happy on the Ormeau Road. There is no grass for cows to eat on the Ormeau Road.'

'I could take my cow to Ormeau Park,' said Bertie.

'No, Bertie,' said Mrs Boggin.

'Oh Bertie, I'm so sorry,' said Aunt Amanda.

'No need to worry,' said Mrs Boggin. 'Bertie is very sensible, now that he is getting bigger. He knows that cows don't go for walks in Ormeau Park.'

'Cows would like it!' Bertie insisted.

'No, they wouldn't,' said Mrs Boggin. 'Cows don't like traffic.'

'Never mind,' said Aunt Amanda. 'You can come and visit me some day, and then you'll be able to see your cow.'

'By myself?' said Bertie.

'Why, Bertie?' said Aunt Amanda. 'Why by yourself?'

'If Max knows I've got a cow, he'll want one too,' said Bertie.

'I won't let him have one, Bertie,' said Aunt Amanda. 'You'll be the only Boggin with a cow.'

But the Boggins' Volkswagen went home to Livermore Street *without* a cow in the back seat, and Bertie was very sad about it. He didn't get a chance to tell Max he was the only cow-owner, because Mr

Boggin was doing all the talking, as soon as Bertie and
Mrs Boggin came through the door.

'Hot chocolate on the sofa!' he groaned. 'Cornflakes
blocking up the sink. And the kitchen floor . . .'

'You were supposed to look after them!' said Mrs
Boggin, and she took Bertie straight off upstairs to bed,
out of the way of the battle below.

'Mum,' Bertie said, when his mother was tucking him
up. 'You know you said our baby wouldn't come for
ages yet?'

'Yes, Bertie,' said Mrs Boggin. 'That's right. Ages and
ages.'

'Couldn't I have my cow here *until* the baby comes?'
asked Bertie. 'Instead of waiting to go to Aunt Amanda's to see it? I could keep it in my cupboard. It isn't big
like the elephant would have been. The cow would fit in
my cupboard . . .'

'Not quite, Bertie,' said Mrs Boggin. 'And anyway,
now that I'm getting fatter with our baby inside me, I
don't think I'd be able to walk your cow, when you are
at school, do you?'

'My Ghost would walk the cow,' said Bertie.

'No, Bertie,' said Mrs Boggin. 'I don't think your
Ghost would like that, somehow. And your cow
wouldn't like living in the house.'

'I'd like playing with it,' said Bertie. 'So would the
Ghost.'

'You'll soon have the baby to play with,' said Mrs
Boggin.

29

'I don't know if I want to play with it,' said Bertie. 'Max says babies are soppy.'

'You feel my tummy, Bertie,' said Mrs Boggin, and Bertie did. And right through Mrs Boggin's dress he felt a big K–I–C–K!

'It's a big kicker, this baby!' she said. 'Just like you! Not a soppy baby at all. Much better than a cow.'

'I expect it will be,' said Bertie doubtfully.

BUT . . .

Two days later . . .

. . . the postman brought a big box wrapped up in brown paper, with:

For
MASTER BERTIE BOGGIN
12 LIVERMORE STREET,
OFF ORMEAU ROAD
BELFAST 7

on the front, and on the back it had:

Sender
MISS AMANDA BOGGIN
BONEYBEFORE, TENPENNY LANE
BALLYNAHINCH,
COUNTY DOWN,
NORTHERN IRELAND

and on the side it had:

FRAGILE HANDLE WITH CARE

'It's for me!' shouted Bertie. 'I know it is for me because that is my name on the label. BERTIE BOGGIN.'

'There's another label on the side,' said Elsie, poking at the paper.

'It says "Livestock enclosed!" ' said Max, in a puzzled voice.

'Livestock?' said Elsie.

'What's livestock?' said Bertie.

'Oh, animals,' said Mrs Boggin. 'Pigs and bulls and horses and things like that.'

'In *that*?' said Max.

'It's just a wee parcel for Bertie,' said Elsie.

'It's a big big BIG parcel!' said Bertie, and he bounced down to the kitchen to open it, and then he bounced back up again to the front room, because he wasn't allowed to cut string himself, and he couldn't squeeze if off.

'I know what it is!' said the Ghost. 'I know! I know!'

Mrs Boggin cut the string for Bertie, and he pulled back the paper, and lifted the lid of the box inside the paper and there was . . .

'My Special Cow!' said Bertie, holding it in both hands.

It was made of china, shiny black with a white nose, with bright eyes and a big bottom. Bertie put it on the shelf beside his bed, where he could see it every night before he went to sleep.

' "A Moo–Moo for little Bertie," ' read the Ghost, from the label round the cow's neck.

'I'm not little, and it's not a Moo–Moo!' said Bertie.

'It comes to the same thing in the end!' said the Ghost, who liked bright shiny china cows, and wouldn't have minded having one in his coal shed, to keep the picture of Florence Nightingale company.

Chapter Four

Birthday Bubbles

Mr Boggin stayed very grumpy all the week, long after Mrs Boggin had cleared up the burnt tapioca in the kitchen and the place where Max dropped the oil, and given up trying to unglug the sewing machine Max had tried to fix, when she was in Ballynahinch.

'What did you do to him?' she asked Max and Elsie.

'Nothing,' said Elsie.

'We were dead good,' said Max.

'Give or take a few disasters!' said Elsie, who hadn't yet told her Mum about the hole in the sitting-room carpet or what Max did to the washing machine.

'Well, something's the matter with him!' said Mrs Boggin, and the next time he grumped, she asked him what it was.

'Getting old,' said Mr Boggin.

'You're not old!' said Mrs Boggin.

'But I soon will be,' said Mr Boggin.

'I know!' said Mrs Boggin. 'It's your birthday, isn't it? Next week. That's why you're grumpy.'

'Hmmph!' said Mr Boggin, and he grumped off to Ormeau Park to walk Tojo.

'Your Daddy is grumpy because it is almost his birthday,' said Mrs Boggin to Max and Elsie and Bertie, who had been keeping out of the way of Boggin–grumps.

'I'm not grumpy when it's my birthday,' said Bertie. 'I like my birthday.'

'You haven't had as many birthdays as your Daddy has, Bertie,' said Mrs Boggin. 'We'll all have to make a special effort to cheer him up. Nice presents, and a cake . . .'

'A cake with candles!' said Bertie. 'My Ghost can help him blow them out.'

'I wouldn't mention your Ghost, Bertie, if I were you,' said Mrs Boggin. 'But we'll certainly have a cake with candles.'

'How many candles?' said Bertie.

'Wait and see,' said Mrs Boggin, and, the day before Mr Boggin's birthday, she showed Bertie the cake, so that he could count the candles.

'One, two, three . . . four!' said Bertie, counting the candles carefully, because he wasn't very good at counting. 'Daddy is four years old!' he announced.

'You're *five*, Bertie,' said Max. 'Daddy is *much* older.'

'Is he twelve?' asked Bertie, who knew how to make a 12, because it was a 1 and a 2.

'At least,' said Mrs Boggin. 'That's what makes him grumpy.'

Bertie went out to the coal shed to tell the Ghost. The Ghost knew a lot of old people, so he was very interested in ages.

'Daddy is at least twelve,' Bertie told the Ghost.

'I think he might be older,' said the Ghost. 'Twelve isn't very old for a Daddy.'

'Twelve is *very* old,' said Bertie. 'And *at least* twelve is even older.'

'It all depends on your point of view,' said the Ghost, who was much older than twelve. 'What are you getting your Daddy for his birthday, Bertie?'

'I don't know,' said Bertie. 'But I'll get him something Special, to stop him grumping!' And he went back into the house to talk to Mrs Boggin about it.

'You and Max and Elsie are clubbing together to get your Daddy some warm slippers, Bertie,' said Mrs Boggin.

'Brilliant!' said Bertie, who was very pleased with the idea.

'The slippers won't really be from Bertie because he hasn't any money,' said Max. 'It is all our money, not Bertie's!'

'Bertie isn't getting Daddy a present at all!' said Elsie.

'Max!' said Mrs Boggin. 'Elsie!'

'OK,' said Max. 'We'll *pretend* the slippers are from Bertie as well.'

'But we'll know they really aren't!' said Elsie.

They all went to bed, but Bertie couldn't get to sleep. He was worried about his Daddy's birthday present.

Max and Elsie were right. The slippers weren't really from him at all. 'I want to get my Daddy a present from *me*,' Bertie decided.

Just then, the Ghost came gliding up the drainpipe from the yard and slipped into Bertie's room, to say goodnight, before going off on his evening's Haunt at the Spectre's Arms.

'You look worried, Bertie,' the Ghost said.

'I want a nice birthday present for my Daddy, just from me, and *not* from Max and Elsie,' Bertie said.

'Daddies like presents,' the Ghost said.

'What sort of presents?' Bertie asked.

'Motor cars and yachts,' said the Ghost.

'I don't think I could manage those,' Bertie said.

'Gloves and scarves and ties and pipes,' said the Ghost. 'It all depends on how much money you have got to buy the present with.'

'I haven't got any money,' said Bertie sadly.

'Then you won't be able to get your Daddy a present,' said the Ghost.

But . . . next day . . . just before the birthday tea . . . Bertie had an idea!

When all the food was eaten, and the candles puffed, and Mr Boggin came to open his presents, there was an extra one wrapped up in the back page of the *Belfast Telegraph*.

Mr Boggin opened the parcel. 'It's a pipe!' he exclaimed.

'The Ghost said pipes were proper birthday presents,'

Bertie explained. 'And I wanted to get you a proper birthday present to stop you being a sad grumpy!'

'Oh!' said Mr Boggin. 'Thank you, Bertie! I promise I won't be sad and grumpy again!'

'I would, if I got that!' said Elsie, looking at the pipe.

'It's Bertie's old bubble pipe!' Max exclaimed. 'It's not a proper pipe. It's just for bubbles!'

'I'm very pleased with Bertie's present!' said Mr Boggin quickly. 'Thank you very very much, Bertie. A bubble pipe is just what I wanted!'

'Daddy was just being nice to you, Bertie,' said Max, when they were going upstairs to bed.

'Imagine giving a grown-up a bubble pipe!' said Elsie.

'Daddy said he liked it!' said Bertie.

'Daddy would,' said Max.

'Daddy is like that,' said Elsie.

'A rotten old bubble pipe!' said Max.

38

Bertie was very upset.

He went into his own room, and started taking his clothes off. Then the Ghost glided in.

'What's the matter this time, Bertie?' the Ghost asked.

Bertie told him all about Daddy's birthday, and the bubble pipe.

'Very good idea, Bertie!' said the Ghost.

'Daddy said he liked it,' said Bertie. 'I expect he did, don't you?'

'Y-e-s,' said the Ghost. 'Daddies don't use bubble pipes *much*, but I expect he liked it.'

'Very much?' said Bertie hopefully.

'Well, *much*, anyway,' said the Ghost, who didn't want to add the 'very' because he always tried to tell the truth, and he wasn't at all certain about Daddies and bubble pipes.

The Ghost glided back down the drainpipe, heading for his coal shed. On the way down he had to zoom past the bathroom window and, as he did so, he looked in.

Then he ZOOOMED straight back up again to Bertie's room.

'Bertie! Bertie!' said the Ghost, bouncing up and down on the end of Bertie's bed like a man on a trampoline.

'What?' said Bertie sleepily.

'Your Daddy's in the bath, blowing bubbles!' said the Ghost. 'He's using your pipe. There are big bubbles everywhere, all over the bathroom!'

'I knew he would like my pipe!' said Bertie, sitting up. 'Max! Elsie! Daddy is using my bubble pipe in his birthday bath. I *told* you he liked it. I told you it was a proper present.'

But Max and Elsie were fast asleep, and didn't hear him.

'Never mind,' said the Ghost.

'Bubbles!' said Bertie happily. 'Birthday Bubbles!'

Chapter Five

The Boggin Art Exhibition

One day the postman came while the Boggins were having breakfast. He gave Mr Boggin a lot of letters.

'Electricity bill!' Mr Boggin grumbled. 'Coal bill. Reminder about the rates. And there is one here for Elsie.'

'Let me see!' said Max, grabbing the important-looking envelope.

'Max!' said Mrs Boggin. 'That's for Elsie!'

And so it was.

The envelope was addressed:

MISS ELSIE BOGGIN
12 LIVERMORE STREET,
BELFAST

and marked 'PERSONAL'.

Elsie looked at it carefully, and then she put it down beside her plate, and finished her porridge.

'What about your letter, dear?' asked Mrs Boggin.

'It is *my* letter,' said Elsie, and she took it into the

front room to open it, where she could be all-by-herself.

'Wooooooo! YIPPEE!'

There was a shriek, and a bang, and Elsie tore out of the front room, with a rosy-red face and a big smile. She thrust her letter into Mrs Boggin's hand.

'I've won a PRIZE!' Elsie exclaimed. 'My painting has won a prize in the Art Competition!'

'Oh well done, Elsie!' said Mr Boggin.

'Aren't you the clever girl?' said Mrs Boggin. 'You're a real wee artist now!'

'Like me,' said Bertie. 'I won a prize at sand designing, didn't I?'

'Yes, Bertie,' said Mrs Boggin. 'You did.'

'Sand designing is kid's stuff,' said Max scornfully. 'And I bet Elsie's rotten old picture wasn't much good either!'

'Max!' said Mrs Boggin.

'Well, I can paint better than stupid Elsie any day!' said Max.

'Do it then!' said Elsie. 'We'll have a Painting Exhibition, and see who's the best.'

They both went off upstairs to get their paints. Soon they were hard at work.

'I want to paint too,' said Bertie. 'I am a good artist, amn't I, Mum?'

'All right, Bertie,' said Mrs Boggin, and she put a special apron on Bertie and set him down at the kitchen table with his paintbox and brush, and an eggcup full of water.

Bertie started to paint.

Elsie came through the room, on her way to get some more water.

'You can't *paint*!' she said scornfully to Bertie.

Bertie stuck his tongue out at her.

It was bright green.

'Mum!' Elsie shouted. 'Bertie's turning green.'

Mrs Boggin rushed into the room.

'Stick your tongue out, Bertie,' Elsie said.

'Can't!' Bertie mumbled.

'Why not?' said Elsie.

'Because it's rude!' said Bertie.

'You did it a minute ago,' said Elsie.

'A minute ago I *meant* to be rude,' said Bertie. 'I was being rude to you, because you were rude to me.'

'Tongue out, Bertie!' ordered Mrs Boggin.

Bertie stuck his tongue out.

43

'Eugh!' said Mrs Boggin, and she spent the next five minutes getting green paint off Bertie's tongue, though he was still a little green around the gums when she had finished.

'Don't lick your brush again, Bertie!' Mrs Boggin ordered, and she went off about her work.

Bertie started painting.

SWIOOOSHHH!

Bertie's eggcup full of paint-water spilled all over the table, and the water dripped down on Tojo, who woke up to find his nose turning purple.

'Bertie!' cried Mrs Boggin.

'I didn't mean to knock it over, Mum!' wailed Bertie, as his mother advanced on him.

Tojo scrambled out from underneath the table, leaving a trail of purple footprints across the floor, on his way to find somewhere quiet where he could worry about purple noses. He'd had a nice black shiny nose for years, and he was too old to take the change easily.

'No more painting today, Bertie,' said Mrs Boggin, removing Bertie to the bathroom. His hands were red, blue and yellow, and some of his hair had taken on a whitish tint that made him look a little like a snowman.

Mrs Boggin spent quite a long time paint-stripping Bertie and the kitchen lino and Tojo, not to mention the chair Bertie had been sitting on. She had just collapsed in the kitchen with a cup of tea when Max came bouncing down the stairs.

'It's Exhibition Time!' Max shouted, galloping into the kitchen. 'You are to judge the best, Mum! We've done lots and lots of pictures, and they're all hung up for you to see!'

There were five paintings on the chest of drawers, next to Max's room on the landing upstairs. Beside them was a big card which said:

PAINTINGS EXHIBITED BY MAXIMILIAN BOGGIN
ARTIST AND MAN OF LETTERS

'That just means he can read,' said Elsie scornfully. And five more outside Elsie's room, with a sign that said:

PAINTINGS EXHIBITED BY E. M. BOGGIN
ART COMPETITION PRIZE WINNER

'Baby-doodles!' said Max scornfully.
'Baby-doodler yourself!' said Elsie.
'Children!' said Mrs Boggin.
'Well, he is!' said Elsie. 'I'm the real painter in this house, the one who wins prizes.'

'I painted a picture too!' Bertie said, puffing up the stairs with his picture under his arm. He got Max's drawing pins, and pinned it up outside his room.

'That's my picture!' he said proudly, but nobody was paying any attention.

'Mine are best, Mum, aren't they?' Max said, and then he added persuasively: 'The one with the big ears is *you*.'

'She hasn't got big ears,' said Elsie.

'Yes she has. Haven't you, Mum?' said Max.

'If you say so, dear,' said Mrs Boggin, looking not too pleased.

'And a big tummy,' said Bertie. 'Very big.'

'Y-e-s,' said Mrs Boggin. 'That's our baby, getting bigger.'

'It is much bigger than it used to be,' said Bertie.

'That's enough about my tummy,' said Mrs Boggin. 'This is *supposed* to be an Art Exhibition, Bertie, not a Tummy Club.'

'Which painting is *best*, Mum?' said Elsie, who was almost sure hers was, but wanted to have her mother say so.

'All of mine are better than all of yours!' said Max. 'And Bertie's too!'

'Mum's the judge, not you!' said Elsie.

'W-e-l-l . . .' said Mrs Boggin doubtfully. 'I think . . . I think there ought to be Special Categories, you see. There always are, in Art Exhibitions. I think Max is best in the Senior Boys, and Elsie is best in the Senior Girls.'

'Oh,' said Max and Elsie.

'What about me?' said Bertie. 'What am I best in?'

'Making a mess!' said Mrs Boggin, but Bertie looked so disappointed that she added hurriedly: 'You win the Little Boy's Prize, Bertie.'

'What is it?' asked Bertie.

'I . . . I . . . a sweetie. You win a sweetie, Bertie,' said Mrs Boggin, and she gave him one.

'Bertie's painting is just a splash!' said Elsie, when Mrs Boggin had gone back downstairs. 'He spilled his water all over it. He doesn't deserve a prize.'

'Silly soppy kid!' said Max.

And they went off downstairs, to see what the Senior Girls' and Senior Boys' Prizes were, in case Mrs Boggin forgot about having to present them.

Going down the stairs, they stepped straight through the Ghost, who was sitting peacefully reading about Ghost Holidays in the *Evening Haunt*. The Ghost was quite flustered. He came gliding up the stairs, and found Bertie gazing at the Art Exhibition.

'I don't think much of that!' said the Ghost, looking at the picture of Mrs Boggin with big ears, painted by Max.

'Elsie's are nice,' said Bertie. 'Elsie won the Senior Girls.'

'Not to my taste,' said the Ghost, moving along the line of paintings in the Exhibition. 'I can't say that I really like any of these. I . . . OH I SAY!'

He had stopped in front of Bertie's picture, pinned up on the wall.

'Now *that*, THAT, Bertie, is a very beautiful picture indeed. Very fine. I wonder who did that one? It is absolutely the best in the whole Exhibition.'

'That's mine,' said Bertie proudly.

'Well! My goodness, Bertie! It is the best picture of a splash I have ever seen.'

'A splash?' said Bertie.

'A perfect splash,' said the Ghost. 'Just like the real thing!'

'I'm rather good at painting splashes, amn't I?' Bertie said modestly. 'I think I'm best at splashes, really. I'm not very good at people.'

'Pictures of people are old-fashioned,' said the Ghost, who was very fond of his picture of Florence Nightingale, but otherwise didn't like people-pictures much, unless they were of nurses or heroes.

'Bertie . . . could I . . . could I possibly have your Picture of a Splash to hang on my coal shed wall?' asked the Ghost hopefully.

'Of course!' said Bertie.

And there it hangs to this day, where the Ghost can see it when he wakes up in the morning, and last thing at night when he's come home from haunting, and is ready to flop down in bed.

It is a very splash-like picture indeed, which is hardly surprising in the circumstances.

The Boggin Art Exhibition

by B.BOGGIN 12 LiVeRMore
street Belfast

(The paw print is by Tojo Boggin,
short for Thomas Joseph.)

Chapter Six

The Ghost Gets Hoovered Up

One morning, Mr and Mrs Boggin got up very early, and started making lists.

'What are you making lists about, Mum?' Bertie asked.

'Baby-buying!' said Mrs Boggin.

'Oh,' said Bertie. 'I didn't know we had to *buy* it. Will it cost a lot of money?'

'Lots!' said Mr Boggin, but Mrs Boggin laughed and said: 'Not the baby, Bertie. We don't have to buy the baby. Just things *for* the baby, so we'll have everything ready when it comes.'

'What sort of everything?' asked Bertie. 'Toys?'

'The baby will be too small for toys to begin with, Bertie,' said Mrs Boggin.

'If you bought it toys, I could play with them until the baby is big enough,' said Bertie hopefully.

'Well, we'll see,' said Mrs Boggin. 'First we've got to get nappies and clothes and bottles to feed the baby with, and lots and lots of other things that babies need.'

'Did I need them?' said Bertie.

'Yes,' said Mrs Boggin.

'But your mother gave them all away,' said Mr Boggin. 'So now we've got to get new ones.'

'New ones to be nice for the baby!' said Bertie.

'That's right!' said Mrs Boggin.

'You'll have to spend all your money!' said Bertie.

'That's right too!' groaned Mr Boggin.

'Will there be enough left for us?' said Bertie anxiously.

'Yes,' said Mrs Boggin. 'Don't worry about it, Bertie. It's all planned.'

'Good,' said Bertie.

And he went out to the coal shed to tell the Ghost.

'Mum and Daddy are going out to spend all our money on things for the baby,' Bertie said.

'Babies often work that way,' said the Ghost.

'But I'm not to worry about it, because it is All Planned,' said Bertie.

'I'm sure your Mummy and Daddy have worked everything out very carefully, Bertie,' said the Ghost. 'Mummies and Daddies are very careful about that sort of thing and you've got a very careful Mummy and Daddy.'

Mr and Mrs Boggin got into the Volkswagen and went off, and Mrs Cafferty from next door came in to look after Max and Elsie and Bertie.

'I don't need looking after,' Max told her. 'I can look after myself.'

'I'm sure you can, Maximilian,' said Mrs Cafferty.

'We both can,' said Elsie.

'But then there's Bertie,' said Mrs Cafferty. 'Bertie needs baby-sat, because he is small. I'm really here to look after Bertie, and you can help me.'

So Max and Elsie helped Mrs Cafferty to look after Bertie.

Max tidied up Bertie's jigsaw puzzle, when Bertie was half-way through it, and Elsie washed Bertie's face, several times, with lots of soap that got in his eyes, and Max put Bertie's motor car on the mantelpiece where he couldn't reach it and Elsie got the scrubbing brush and . . .

'Elsie!' said Mrs Cafferty. 'What are you doing to poor little Bertie?'

52

'Scrubbing him,' said Elsie.

'I don't want to be scrubbed,' said Bertie.

'No scrubbing, Elsie,' said Mrs Cafferty.

'And Max put my motor car where I can't get it!' said Bertie.

'Max, return that motor car to the floor at once!' said Mrs Cafferty.

'You said we should help you to look after him,' said Max.

'Well, you've helped enough for one day,' said Mrs Cafferty. 'I'll do the rest of the looking after Bertie all by myself, thank you very much.'

Mrs Cafferty played Pin Pegs with Bertie, and she helped him look for the bit of his jigsaw Max had lost when he was tidying up, and she watched cartoons with him, and then she got fed up, and decided to make herself a cup of tea.

'You play by yourself for a minute, Bertie,' she said.

'I'll play with my Ghost,' Bertie said, and he went out to the back yard.

'Ghost?' said Mrs Cafferty.

'Bertie's got a ghost he plays with,' said Elsie. 'It isn't a real ghost. It's one he makes up. He plays with it in the . . .' she was going to say 'coal shed', but then she didn't.

'*Outside*,' she said carefully, and she went upstairs and got the scrubbing brush and the soap ready.

Mrs Cafferty had a cup of tea and read her book and borrowed four of Mrs Boggin's best biscuits, and then she went to the kitchen to wash the tea things.

She looked out into the back yard.

A little coaly person was standing there, talking to the wall.

'Bertie!' cried Mrs Cafferty. 'You're . . . you're all covered in coal!'

'Am I?' said Bertie.

'Oh Bertie,' said Mrs Cafferty. 'You should never ever play in the coal shed. What a mess!'

'I was playing with my Ghost,' said Bertie.

'I'll have to have a word with your ghost,' said Mrs Cafferty, and she carted Bertie off upstairs, where she found the soap and the scrubbing brush all laid out by Elsie.

Bertie wasn't allowed out in the back yard again, in case he paid another visit to the coal shed.

So the Ghost came in.

'Good afternoon,' the Ghost said to Mrs Cafferty, taking off his hat very politely, but he might as well not have bothered, because Mrs Cafferty didn't believe in ghosts, and so she didn't see him.

'Hmmmh!' said the Ghost. 'Not very polite, I must say.'

Then Mrs Cafferty sat on the Ghost.

It wasn't her fault. She didn't know that he had settled in the big armchair, beside the fire. The coal shed had become a little chilly, and the Ghost always liked to come in and sit for a while, but he didn't like being sat on.

'Pardon me!' said the Ghost, standing up, but what

he really meant was 'I-Pardon-You', although as Mrs Cafferty didn't hear him, it didn't make any difference.

'You sat on my Ghost,' Bertie told Mrs Cafferty.

'Oh dear,' said Mrs Cafferty. 'Where is he?'

'There,' said Bertie, pointing at the safe place behind the curtains where he couldn't be sat on, which the Ghost had just slipped into.

'I'm so sorry, Ghost,' said Mrs Cafferty. 'Do accept my apologies!'

'Certainly, Madam,' said the Ghost.

'He says he does,' said Bertie.

'Your ghost must be a perfect gentleman,' said Mrs Cafferty.

'He is,' said Bertie.

Then Mrs Cafferty looked at her watch, and said, 'Oh heavens!' and started tidying up.

'What are you tidying up for?' Bertie asked.

'Because the place has got a bit messy with all our games, Bertie,' said Mrs Cafferty. 'And I don't want your Mummy to have a lot of work to do when she comes in, poor dear.'

'Don't tidy up my Ghost,' said Bertie.

'I won't,' said Mrs Cafferty.

But she did.

When she got Max's skates out from behind the curtain, she *bumped* the Ghost.

'You bumped him!' said Bertie.

'So sorry!' said Mrs Cafferty.

Then she got the brush, to clear up the coal-dust that had fallen off Bertie when he was on his way upstairs.

'Ooooh!' wailed the Ghost.

'Now you've brushed him!' reported Bertie.

'I didn't!' said Mrs Cafferty.

'You did!' said Bertie.

The coal-dust wouldn't come off the carpet, so Mrs Cafferty got the Hoover.

Voooooooooooom! went the Hoover.

'Aaaaaaaaahhhhhhhhhh!' wailed the Ghost.

'Oh no!' cried Bertie.

Vooooooooom! Mrs Cafferty hoovered on. She

couldn't hear Bertie, because of the noise the Hoover was making, and she couldn't hear the Ghost, but Bertie could.

'H–e–l–p!' the Ghost cried.

'Stop! Stop! STOP, MRS CAFFERTY!' Bertie shouted.

Mrs Cafferty stopped, and switched off.

'You hoovered my Ghost!' said Bertie accusingly.

'I never did!' said Mrs Cafferty.

'Yes you did. You hoovered him right up into your bag. He was sitting very peacefully on the pouffe, having a snooze, and you hoovered him right up.'

'Oh Bertie!' said Mrs Cafferty. 'I'm so sorry! What shall we do?'

'Better empty him out, quickly!' said Bertie.

So Bertie and Mrs Cafferty went out to the back yard, and Mrs Cafferty opened the Hoover and took out the bag . . .

. . . and the Ghost came out of it.

'Ooooooh!' shuddered the Ghost.

Dust was all over him. When he moved, it floated in all directions.

'Ecuh! Ecuh! Ecuh!' hiccupped the Ghost, heading for his coal shed.

'Is he all right?' asked Mrs Cafferty.

'I don't think so,' said Bertie. 'I'll just go in and see!'

'Oh no you won't!' said Mrs Cafferty, swiftly, because she wasn't going to allow Bertie back in the coal shed.

'But the Ghost . . .'

'The Ghost Game does not include going back into

the coal shed, Bertie!' said Mrs Cafferty, and she hauled
Bertie back inside.

Bertie was very cross.

'It isn't a game!' he told Mrs Cafferty, but she didn't
pay any attention.

Then Mr and Mrs Boggin came back with the
Volkswagen filled up with baby-parcels, and everybody
spent ages opening the parcels and having more cups of
tea, and then Mrs Cafferty said how-good-the-children-
have-been and went home.

'Well, Bertie,' said Mrs Boggin, when Mrs Cafferty had
gone. 'Did you have a good time while we were out?'

'No,' said Bertie.

'Oh!' said Mrs Boggin.

And Bertie told her all about the Hoovered Ghost.

'Oh dear!' said Mrs Boggin. 'I bet he wasn't pleased.'

'He went "Ecuh! Ecuh! Ecuh!" ' said Bertie. 'I expect it was all the dust he'd swallowed.'

'I expect it was,' said Mrs Boggin.

'I'll just go out and see if he's all right,' said Bertie.

But when he went out to the coal shed, the Ghost wasn't there. Beneath the sign

BEWARE OF THE GHOST

which the Ghost had put up on the coal shed wall, there was another sign which said:

GONE TO THE SPECTRE'S ARMS

BACK SOON

But the Ghost wasn't Back Soon. He still wasn't back when Bertie went to bed, and he didn't turn up until after Mrs Boggin had switched out the light and kissed Bertie goodnight.

Then . . .

. . . slowly . . .

. . . the curtains stirred . . .

and a still-a-bit-dusty Ghost emerged from behind them.

'Is she gone, Bertie?' he asked. 'The woman with the Hoover. Is she gone?'

'Yes, Ghost,' said Bertie.

'Not hiding anywhere?' said the Ghost. 'Not . . . not hoovering?'

'Gone home,' said Bertie.

'Good,' said the Ghost, and he plopped down on the chair by Bertie's bed.

'What a day!' he said. 'What-a-day! Ghosts have been in tight corners before, like the Charge of the Light Brigade, and the Battle of Balaclava, and being sat upon in buses, but never, never a corner like that.'

'What was it like?' said Bertie.

'Hot!' said the Ghost. 'Hot and dusty! One minute I was snoozing on the pouffe and the next, without even time to shrink or get away, I was all sucked up!'

'I'm very sorry, Ghost,' said Bertie.

'It wasn't your fault,' said the Ghost, who was a very forgiving Ghost. 'But I wish people would learn to be a little more careful.'

'Like my Mummy and Daddy,' said Bertie.

'Exactly,' said the Ghost. 'In all the time I have been here, your Mummy hasn't hoovered me once.'

'Neither has my Daddy,' said Bertie.

'I don't think your Daddy uses the Hoover much,' said the Ghost. And he wisped back down the drain-pipe to the coal shed to have a little rest and recover from Bertie-Being-Baby-Sat.

Chapter Seven

Bertie and the Bad Witch

'It will soon be baby-time!' Mr Boggin went around boasting to everyone.

'The sooner the better!' said Mrs Boggin.

All the Boggins agreed with her because, as Mrs Boggin got fatter and fatter, she wanted to sit down with her feet up most of the day.

Things didn't get done.

Even the Ghost got fed up.

'I'm not at all sure about this new baby, Bertie,' the Ghost said. 'The house is all dusty, and it makes me sneeze.'

Bertie told his Mum.

'Tell the Ghost "tough luck" and why doesn't he clean the house himself?' said Mrs Boggin.

'The Ghost says his coal shed is clean,' said Bertie.

'Then he can just sit in it!' said Mrs Boggin.

Bertie told the Ghost.

'I don't think that that is very nice,' said the Ghost.

'People ought to be polite to ghosts, considering all ghosts have to put up with, with new babies on the way.'

'What do ghosts have to put up with?' asked Bertie.

'Dust!' said the Ghost. 'And dishes undone. And not so many nice cooking smells, since your Dad started doing the dinners and . . .'

'And what?' said Bertie.

'You haven't got so much time to play with me,' said the Ghost. 'You're always getting things for your Mum.'

'Mum needs me,' said Bertie. 'I'm her special helper.'

'Hmmmph!' grumbled the Ghost. 'Nobody has any time for me.'

Bertie told Max and Elsie. 'You've all got to be nice to my Ghost!' he said. 'My Ghost is feeling lonely, because I'm not able to play with him so much.'

'We don't believe in ghosts,' said Elsie.

'Silly old ghosts!' said Max.

And he made up a song about ghosts, and went out to sing it in the back yard, so that the Ghost could hear him, if there *was* a ghost, although he thought there wasn't. Really, he just wanted to annoy Bertie.

'Ghosts are fat,
Ghosts are silly,
Ghosts have bottoms
That get chilly!'

sang Max.

'Stop it! Stop it! Stop it!' shouted Bertie, who was afraid that the Ghost would get really cross, and go to live somewhere else.

'Ghosts are like
Big fat custard.
Fill them up
With stingy mustard!'

sang Max.
'STOP IT!' wailed Bertie.

'Ghosts are gross,
Ghosts are smellies,
Not like roses,
Like my wellies!'

sang Max.
That was when *Somebody* turned on the hose.
The hose had been lying curled up at the coal shed door, and *Somebody* turned on the tap. The hose twitched and . . .

'Ghosts are bullies,
Ghosts are thugs,
Ghosts are silly billy
Mu . . .'

W–O–O–O–S–H! went the hose.

'Yaaaaah!' yelled Max, as the water spurted all over him.

'Ha! Ha!' went Bertie. 'You're all wet!'

'I'll . . . I'll . . .' stuttered Max, and then he charged at Bertie, waving his fists.

'NO!' wailed Bertie.

And Mrs Cafferty heard him.

There was a big row!

'You must learn to be more considerate, Max,' Mrs Cafferty said. 'Your mother needs all her strength for the new baby, not chasing after you.'

'Who is going to look after us, then?' said Max, dripping and sniffing.

'Your Aunt Amanda will when the time comes,' said Mrs Cafferty. 'Meanwhile *you* can help everyone by looking after Elsie and Bertie.'

'He's not looking after me,' said Elsie quickly. 'He's a drip!'

'Who are you calling a drip?' Max said.

And they both got into trouble with Mrs Cafferty.

'Serve you right!' said Bertie.

'I don't like Mrs Cafferty!' muttered Max. 'She's not my Mum!'

'I *hate* her,' said Elsie. 'She's . . . she's a Bad Old Witch, that's what she is.'

'Ooooh!' said Bertie. 'Is she?'

Elsie stomped off into the kitchen, leaving Bertie looking very worried.

'I'm going to tell Mum!' he said, and he went to look for her, but he couldn't find her in the living room, where she usually lay down. Instead, Mr Boggin was there, cleaning up.

'Don't disturb your mother!' said Mr Boggin. 'She's upstairs resting.'

'Daddy,' said Bertie. 'Daddy, Elsie says Mrs Cafferty is a . . .'

That was when Mr Boggin realized that Bertie was covered in coal-dust from the back yard.

'I told you not to play in that coal shed, Bertie!' he said.

'The Ghost said I could,' said Bertie.

'There's no time for your Ghost games, with a new baby on the way!' said Mr Boggin, and the usual happened. Bertie was carried off upstairs by Elsie, and de-coaled from ankle to eyebrow.

A little while later a clean Bertie went out to the back yard, where Max was mending a puncture in his football.

'Max,' said Bertie. 'Elsie says that Mrs Cafferty is a Bad Witch.'

'I thought everyone knew that,' said Max casually. 'Didn't you know, little Bertie?'

'No, I didn't,' said Bertie anxiously. He didn't like the idea of having a Bad Witch in the house next door who sometimes came in and Bertie-sat when Mum was having her Baby-rest.

'I'll show you something,' said Max, and he took Bertie out through the yard door, and along the alley to Mrs Cafferty's, where he opened *her* yard door, a little. 'Mrs Cafferty has a black hat and broomstick and flies around the Ormeau Road all night, as far down as the Gas-works, and as far up as Carryduff!' said Max. 'Just you look inside there, Bertie, and see what you can see.'

Bertie peered round the door.

'Go on,' said Max, and Bertie stepped inside.

SLAM!

Max slammed the door shut.

Bertie was trapped in the Bad Witch's back yard.

'Maaaaaax!' wailed Bertie.

Then Mrs Cafferty's kitchen door opened, and the Bad Witch came through it.

Bertie couldn't escape.

'Bertie Boggin!' said Mrs Cafferty. 'Wee Bertie Boggin! What are you doing in *my* back yard, Bertie Boggin?'

'I . . . I . . . I . . .' began Bertie, and then he stopped, and gulped, and said: 'Are you a *Witch*?'

'A witch?' said Mrs Cafferty.

'A B . . . B . . . B . . . *Bad* Witch?' said Bertie, and then he added, 'Max and Elsie say you are, but I don't believe them.'

'Well now,' said Mrs Cafferty. 'As a matter of fact, Bertie Boggin, and just between you and me and our car, I *am* one.'

'A Witch?' gasped Bertie. 'A *Bad* Witch?'

'No,' said Mrs Cafferty. 'A *Good* Witch.'

Bertie thought about it. A Good Witch was better to have as a next-door neighbour than a Bad Witch, but any Witch at all . . .

'I do *good* things,' said Mrs Cafferty. 'I make boys and girls happy.'

'Oh,' said Bertie. That sounded a lot better.

'I *quite* like Good Witches,' he added.

'Wait a minute, Bertie,' Mrs Cafferty said, and she went back into the house. When she came back again she said: 'Hocus–Pocus–Dot–A–Docus! What have we here?' And she put her hand into Bertie's ear, and pulled out a sweet.

'Oh!' gasped Bertie.

'It always works,' said Mrs Cafferty.

'What does?' said Bertie.

'Hocus–Pocus–Dot–A–Docus!' said Mrs Cafferty. 'That's a Magic Witch spell. Very magic. You can try it if you like.'

'I'm not a Witch,' said Bertie.

'It will probably work for you just the same,' said Mrs Cafferty. 'You look a Magic sort of person to me.'

'Hocus–Pocus–Dot–A–Docus!' went Bertie, and he stuck his finger in his ear, but there wasn't a sweetie there.

'No sweet,' he said. 'Didn't work!'

'Wait . . . wait . . . it's coming!' said Mrs Cafferty. 'The sweetie is coming.'

'Where?' said Bertie.

'*There!*' said Mrs Cafferty, opening her hand. 'There you are, Bertie. You magicked three sweeties into my hand.' And she gave them to him.

Bertie went back to the Boggins', clutching the sweets.

'Ghost! Ghost!' he called, running into the back yard. 'I magicked, Hocus–Pocus–Dot–A–Docus! That's a Magic Witch spell and I magicked it, I magicked a whole sweet.'

'Did you, Bertie?' said the Ghost, sounding most impressed. 'Well I never.'

'A Good Witch taught me!' said Bertie. He didn't tell the Ghost who the Good Witch was, because the Ghost didn't like talking about Mrs Cafferty, since he'd been hoovered. Even *thinking* about Mrs Cafferty was enough to make him run away and hide on top of the coal heap, where the Hoover was unlikely to go.

'Well done,' said the Ghost admiringly. 'Witches usually have to be quite experienced before they get round to magicking things.'

'I expect it's because I'm a Magic sort of person,' said Bertie, remembering what Mrs Cafferty had told him.

'And you've mixed with some very Magic ghosts,' said the Ghost modestly.

'Y-e-s,' said Bertie, who didn't think his Magic Words had anything much to do with the Ghost, but didn't like to say so.

'Who is the Witch, Bertie?' the Ghost asked.

'Mrs Cafferty,' said Bertie.

There was a long pause.

'Oh well,' said the Ghost. 'I suppose that shouldn't surprise me in the least. If she can hoover a ghost she can do anything.'

'The hoovering was just an accident, Ghost,' said

Bertie. 'Elsie was wrong. Mrs Cafferty isn't a Bad Witch. She's a Good Witch. She goes around making other people happy.'

'*Hoovering* them?' said the Ghost, who didn't think much of being hoovered as a way of being happy.

'N-o,' said Bertie.

'Ah well,' said the Ghost. 'Hocus–Pocus–Dot–A–Docus, I must add that to my list of Magic Words.'

'I don't know if it works for ghosts,' said Bertie, very seriously.

'Ghosts learn to put up with these things,' said the Ghost, and he settled back to suck one of the sweets that Bertie had magicked.

'Hey!' shouted an angry Max from the yard. 'Who let down my football?'

'Not me!' said Bertie.

But the Ghost only grinned.

There are some things ghosts can do *without* magic, and letting down unfriendly people's footballs is one of them.

Chapter Eight

Baby–Beginning Day

The very next day was Baby–beginning Day, but Mr and Mrs Boggin and Max and Elsie and Bertie and the Ghost didn't know about it when they went to bed the night before.

Baby–beginning day didn't begin in the morning; it began in the middle of the night, with Tojo barking so much that he woke Bertie up.

'Ghost?' said Bertie, because usually when he woke up at night it was the Ghost who woke him. But the Ghost wasn't there.

So Bertie went downstairs, and downstairs were Mr and Mrs Boggin and Mrs Cafferty the Good Witch from next door and Essie Smith and a taxi driver.

'Bertie!' said Mrs Boggin, and she gave him a big hug.

'What's the matter?' said Bertie.

'Nothing is the matter, wee Bertie!' said Mrs Boggin. 'It's just Baby–beginning Day, and I'm rushing off to the hospital in a taxi so the baby can begin there.'

'Can I rush off with you?' said Bertie.

'No,' said Mrs Boggin. 'You stay here with Mrs Cafferty, Bertie!'

'I'll be back soon, Bertie!' said Mr Boggin, and helped Mrs Boggin into the big black taxi, and they went off down the road, driving very carefully, because of the baby inside Mrs Boggin.

Mrs Cafferty and Essie Smith went back into the Boggins' house, and Mrs Cafferty made Bertie a drink and Essie Smith told him a story, and then Mrs Cafferty put Bertie back to bed.

'Do you know who is coming in the morning, Bertie?' she said.

'The baby?' said Bertie.

'No,' said Mrs Cafferty. 'Probably *not* the baby. The baby is only beginning. It might take a few days. But somebody extra special is coming first thing tomorrow morning to look after you.'

'Aunt Amanda!' said Bertie.

'Right!' said Mrs Cafferty. 'Just right, Bertie Boggin. I knew you'd know, because you are sort of magic, aren't you?'

'Yes,' said Bertie.

And, the very first thing the next morning, the doorbell went Brrrrrnng! Brrrrrng! Brnnnng! and Mrs Cafferty shouted up the stairs, 'Children! Look who's here to see you! Your Aunt Amanda Boggin from Ballynahinch!'

'Sweets!' shouted Max. 'Aunt Amanda always brings sweets!' and he led the charge down the stairs.

'Good morning, Aunt Amanda,' said Elsie, very politely. 'It is very good of you to come so quickly.'

'I hope you are keeping well, Aunt Amanda,' said Max, hovering close to Aunt Amanda's bag.

'Have you got sweeties for us?' asked Bertie.

'Bertie!' said Mrs Cafferty. 'That's terribly rude.'

'Sweeties!' said Aunt Amanda, opening her bag. She picked out a box and emptied some sweets on the table in three piles. 'Who can count them?' she said.

'One, two, three, four, five, six,' said Max, in the voice he kept for not-very-clever aunts who thought children couldn't count.

'One, two, three, four, five,' said Elsie, counting her pile without hesitation.

'And here's one more to make six, so that everyone has the same,' said Aunt Amanda.

'One, two, three, four,' began Bertie. Then he

stopped, and then he said, uncertainly: 'Five. Fourteen. Thirteen.' And he looked anxiously at Aunt Amanda and Mrs Cafferty.

'Well done, Bertie!' said Aunt Amanda, and she gave him another three for counting so well.

Then Aunt Amanda and Mrs Cafferty went to have a cup of tea and talk about babies, and Bertie, who was tired of baby-talking, went out to the back yard to eat his sweets.

'I don't think you counted that *quite* right,' said the Ghost, who had been wisping about the house to see if there was anything he could do to help, whilst at the same time keeping a wary eye out just in case Mrs Cafferty decided to hoover.

Bertie finished the last of his sweets.

'I know,' he said.

'Hmm,' said the Ghost.

'I know, but Aunt Amanda *didn't*, did she?' said Bertie.

'Then she can't count either,' said the Ghost.

'Aunts ought to be able to count,' said Bertie, who thought Aunts were capable of most things.

'Some ghosts are not very good at counting,' said the Ghost. 'Because of the wispy fingers, you know.' He was about to explain how wispy fingers were difficult to count on, when he realized that Bertie wasn't listening.

Bertie had gone back into the house, because he had heard someone say: 'Ice-cream!'

'We'll divide it into three!' said Aunt Amanda, getting

ready to cut the ice-cream block she had brought out of her bag.

'Four,' said Bertie.

'Three,' said Max scornfully. 'Bertie can't count, he's too small.'

'I expect Bertie meant we should give some to Mrs Cafferty,' said Aunt Amanda. 'But Mrs Cafferty has gone back next door now that I've come, and I don't want any, so there's only three pieces needed.'

'*Four*,' said Bertie, a second time.

'One for Max, one for me, one for Bertie,' said Elsie. 'That makes three pieces, doesn't it, Aunt Amanda?'

'One for me,' said Bertie. 'One for Max. One for Elsie . . .'

'That's *three*,' said Max, impatiently. 'Not four!'

'Told you he couldn't count,' said Elsie.

'One for the baby?' said Aunt Amanda brightly. 'But the baby isn't here yet, and when it does come it will be far too small to want any ice-cream, just yet awhile.'

'Not the baby,' said Bertie. 'One for me, one for Max, one for Elsie, and one for the Ghost. That makes four. I *can* count to four, so I know it is four!'

'You little cheat!' said Elsie.

'It's *three*!' said Max. 'Bertie's Ghost doesn't need any ice-cream!'

'Of course we have to have a piece for the Ghost!' exclaimed Aunt Amanda, who knew all about Bertie's Ghost, because Mrs Boggin had given her special Look-after-Bertie-and-his-Ghost orders.

She cut the ice-cream block into four big slices.

'I'll take mine out to the yard, and have it with the Ghost,' Bertie said, and he went out to the back yard with two slices of ice-cream.

'He's going to eat them both!' grumbled Elsie. 'It isn't fair. His ghost is just made up.'

'Bertie gets two of everything, pretending that it is for his ghost,' said Max. 'And there is *no* ghost. It's a rotten swizz!'

'That's enough of that, Max,' said Aunt Amanda.

'We'll catch Bertie at it!' said Max, when Aunt Amanda had gone out of the room. 'We'll catch him eating both ice-creams himself, and that will prove to everyone that there is no ghost!'

They tiptoed out to the yard. Bertie was sitting on the bin beside the coal shed with one empty ice-cream dish beside him.

He was busily eating the *second* ice-cream.

'There you are!' said Max, in triumph. 'Caught you! Caught you right at it, Dirty Bertie! You are eating the ghost's ice-cream yourself, which proves that there is no ghost.'

'The Ghost said I could have it,' said Bertie. 'He says ghosts don't like ice-cream.'

'Don't believe you!' said Max.

'*Why* don't ghosts like ice-cream?' asked Elsie.

'Why don't ghosts like ice-cream?' Bertie asked the Ghost, and he added, 'It isn't me who wants to know, it's Elsie.'

'Ghosts are shivery enough at the best of times,' said the Ghost.

Bertie told Elsie what the Ghost had said.

'I don't think they believed me,' Bertie told the Ghost, when Max and Elsie had gone back into the house to complain to Aunt Amanda.

'Doesn't matter,' said the Ghost. 'After all, you've eaten *both* the ice-creams now, haven't you? And Max and Elsie may know how to count past four, but they don't know much about ghosts, do they? You are the expert on ghosts around here.'

'Yes I am,' said Bertie. 'I know almost everything there is to know about ghosts.'

The Ghost didn't say anything, but he smiled a very Ghosty little smile, as if he could have told Bertie a lot more about ghosts, if he had wanted to.

Chapter Nine

The New Boggin

'We've got our new baby!' Mr Boggin shouted, bouncing down the hall. 'I'm a Daddy! I'm a Daddy!'

'You were a Daddy already,' Bertie said. 'You're my Daddy and Max's and Elsie's.'

'Now I'm four times a Daddy,' said Mr Boggin.

'What sort of baby is it?' asked Elsie. 'A boy, or a girl?'

'Girl!' said Mr Boggin, and he grabbed Aunt Amanda and waltzed her round the kitchen, right through the Ghost, who wasn't quick enough to get out of the way.

'Not another girl!' said Max.

'That makes it two–two!' said Elsie.

'Where is it?' said Bertie. 'I want to see it!'

'Coming Thursday!' said Mr Boggin. 'You'll just have to wait, Bertie Boggin!'

Thursday was a long time coming, and Aunt Amanda and Elsie and Max and Bertie were kept very busy getting–new–baby–ready.

Everybody except the Ghost.

'This house is upside down!' grumbled the Ghost.

'No it isn't,' said Bertie, who was busily painting a picture of a Baby-Splash to hang up over the cot.

'Everybody is dashing about doing things!' said the Ghost, feeling tetchy, and he retired to the coal shed to sulk.

Bertie didn't go out to see him.

The Ghost came back into the house.

Bertie was helping Aunt Amanda to fix up the cot, and he hadn't time to talk to the Ghost. The Ghost went upstairs and lay down in the bath, feeling even sulkier.

Bertie came running into the bathroom to fetch Aunt Amanda's cardigan, but he didn't notice the Ghost. He was too busy.

Then BRNNNG! BRNNNG! BRNNNG! went the
doorbell.

Everybody rushed to the front door, including the
Ghost.

It was Mr Boggin and Mrs Boggin and . . .

. . . THE NEW BABY BOGGIN.

The new baby Boggin was very small. It was the
smallest Boggin Bertie had ever seen.

'Like a peanut,' said Max, looking down at it in its cot.

'Like a doll,' said Elsie.

'Smaller than me!' said Bertie, and Mrs Boggin
hugged him a lot. Then she hugged Max, and Elsie, and
Aunt Amanda, and Mr Boggin, but she didn't hug the
Ghost, because she couldn't see him.

The Ghost felt left out.

He drifted off to the coal shed.

Bertie didn't notice that the Ghost was gone.

He was kept far too busy.

BRNNNG! went the doorbell, and it was Essie Smith
from Number Three, come to see the new baby.

'It is smaller than me,' Bertie told her.

Then BRNNNG! BRNNNG! went the doorbell, and it
was Mrs Cafferty, coming to see the new baby.

'I'm bigger than the baby is!' Bertie told her, proudly.

Then BRNNNG! BRNNNG! BRNNNG! went the
doorbell again, and it was BRNNNGING and
BRNNNGING and BRNNNGING for ages and ages.
People kept coming, and Bertie told them all about how
it felt to be bigger than the baby, and Max kept saying

the new baby looked like a peanut until Elsie told Mrs Boggin and Mrs Boggin told him not to, because babies don't like being called peanuts.

It was a long happy day in the Boggin household, but not for everybody.

Somebody had been absolutely and completely forgotten about. Somebody got very very sad, sitting alone in his coal shed.

'Oh! Oh! Oh!' moaned the Somebody. 'I'm lonely!'

Then the Somebody thought: 'If I count to two hundred on my wispy fingers, Bertie will come and play with me.'

He counted to two hundred, but Bertie didn't come.

'Now he's got the new baby to play with, he'll never play with me again!' moaned the Somebody.

And then . . .

'A ghost who isn't played with might as well go and haunt somewhere else, where he'll be appreciated!' said the Somebody.

And the Somebody started to pack.

He packed his tea caddy and his billycan and his Picture of a Splash and his back numbers of the *Evening Haunt* and lastly, very very carefully, he took down the picture of Florence Nightingale that hung on the coal shed wall. Then, with all his luggage, the Ghost wisped out into the yard.

'Bye-bye, coal shed!' he said.

And –

'Bye-bye, Boggins, see you some time, maybe, if I

happen to be haunting round this way!'

And he drifted towards the yard door.

Then . . .

'Ghost?' Bertie called. 'Ghost?'

The Ghost turned round.

'Ghost?' said Bertie. 'All the people have gone away now, and Mum says you can come in and see the baby.'

'Me?' said the Ghost, still holding on to his pictures and bundles.

'The new baby is smaller than me!' Bertie boasted.

'Most babies are, Bertie,' said the Ghost.

'When it gets bigger, I'll be allowed to play with it,' Bertie said.

'I hope you have a nice time, Bertie,' said the Ghost, and he drifted back towards the yard door.

'Aren't you coming in to see the new baby?' said Bertie.

'I'm really too busy, Bertie,' said the Ghost, with a sniff. 'I've got to find a silly new home for a silly old Ghost!'

And he went out through the yard door, and closed it softly behind him.

'G–H–O–S–T!' wailed Bertie, and Mrs Boggin heard him.

She came out of the kitchen.

'Bertie! Bertie . . . whatever is the matter?' she said.

'My Ghost is gone!' wailed Bertie.

'Nonsense,' said Mrs Boggin.

'He's just gone out the yard door!' said Bertie. 'He's going to find a new place to haunt!'

Mrs Boggin went down the yard, and looked out into the entry. All she could see was rubbish bins, lined up along it, and . . . and a kind of slow-moving flicker, at the far end.

'GHOST!' she shouted. 'Ghost! *Come back at once!*'

'Is he coming?' said Bertie anxiously.

'I think he is,' said Mrs Boggin, who couldn't be sure, although the flicker seemed to be moving in her direction.

'Tell him he's got to come in to see the new baby!' said Bertie.

'Ghost!' said Mrs Boggin. 'You are to come in and see the new baby. And that's an *order*!'

The flicker came through the back gate. That's what Mrs Boggin saw . . . or almost saw, because she couldn't be quite sure.

'Oh, Ghost!' said Bertie happily.

They all went into the house.

'Don't say it is like a peanut!' Bertie warned the Ghost. 'Babies don't like being told they look like peanuts.'

The Ghost bent over the baby's cot.

'Ga-ga-ga-ga-ga!' went the Ghost.

The baby didn't do anything. It was too small to go: 'Gug-gug-gug-gug!' back, the way big babies do, but its little tiny peanut face managed a smile.

'It likes you!' said Bertie.

'That's just *wind*, Bertie,' said the Ghost. 'Babies do that when they have windy tummies.'

'Look!' said Mrs Boggin. 'The baby loves the Ghost. It is all smily.'

'That's just wind,' Bertie said. 'The Ghost told me.'

'Oh!' said Mrs Boggin. 'Quite right! I expect your Ghost knows all about babies, Bertie.'

'Yes, he does,' said Bertie.

'He'll be able to help us look after it,' said Mrs Boggin.

The Ghost shimmered a bit, but Mrs Boggin didn't notice.

'You will stay and help us, Ghost, won't you?' said Mrs Boggin.

'Please, Ghost?' said Bertie.

'Well . . .' said the Ghost. 'If you promise you'll still play with me sometimes, Bertie, I might . . .'

'Of course I will,' said Bertie.

'What did the Ghost say, Bertie?' said Mrs Boggin.

'He says he'll stay, if I promise to play with him sometimes.'

'Tell him I'm very pleased,' said Mrs Boggin. 'The house wouldn't be the same without him. Tell him I'll make sure you play with him every day, and so will Florence.'

'Florence?' said the Ghost, brightening up.

'That's the new baby's name, Ghost,' said Bertie.

'After Florence Nightingale?' said the Ghost, getting excited.

'Did you call our new baby after Florence Nightingale, Mum?' asked Bertie.

'Of course I did!' said Mrs Boggin.

'HIP-YIP-HURRAH!' went the Ghost, and he bounced out to the coal shed to put the tea caddy back on the shelf, and hang Florence Nightingale up on the wall.

'Did you *really* call the new Boggin "Florence" because of Florence Nightingale, Mum?' asked Bertie.

'Well, *no*,' said Mrs Boggin. 'Not exactly. She's called Florence after your grandmother, Bertie.'

'That was a lie!' said Bertie.

'Not *e–x–a–c–t–l–y*,' said Mrs Boggin. 'You see, Florence is called Florence after your grandmother, and your grandmother was called Florence after her mother, and her mother was called Florence after Florence Nightingale, so there!'

'Oh!' said Bertie. 'I'll tell the Ghost.'

'I shouldn't bother, Bertie,' said Mrs Boggin. 'You don't want to confuse him, do you?'

'No,' said Bertie.

'We just want your Ghost to stay, and play with you and Florence,' said Mrs Boggin.

'Right!' said Bertie.

And then he thought about it.

'I don't think my Ghost will ever go, Mum,' he said. 'Not so long as I believe in him.'

'You *and* Florence, Bertie,' said Mrs Boggin.

'And Florence!' said Bertie.

But Florence didn't say a word. She was too little to believe or not believe in ghosts, one way or the other.